Fox Tale

Michael Foreman

Andersen Press • London

Mother always kept us warm and safe. Father went hunting in the night and brought us food at dawn.

I will never forget the first time I peeped outside our den. The air was so fresh it took my breath away.

The birds were singing to the rising sun and a cool breeze rustled the leaves of early spring.

The breeze suddenly became a roaring, rattling whirlwind which raced towards me.

I tumbled back into the safety of our den under the ground and snuggled up to Mother and my brother and sister.

I had heard the whirlwind roaring before but always felt safe in our home.

Later in the day, Mother took us all outside and we lay together in the cover of the bushes and watched the brightly coloured whirlwinds race by.

When spring turned into summer, Mother took us out at night. The whirlwinds were still and the moonlit world was quiet.

She showed us where to find good things to eat. Some food we could just pick up and some we had to climb for. And some we had to catch! She told us never, ever, to go on the tracks of the whirlwinds.

Then, on an evening of
mist and falling leaves, we
went out with Father. The
whirlwinds were still rattling
and roaring but we felt safe
with him.

We went to the place
where the whirlwinds stop.
It was very busy.

We watched and waited,
and then Father's ears pricked
up. A man came towards
us. I wondered how he knew
where we were.

He smiled when he saw
Father, and his smile grew
even wider when he saw us.
He took food from his bag;
some of our favourite things.
It was food Father had often
brought home to us. Now I
knew where it had come from.

Every evening after that,
Father took us to meet the
man, and each time he had
something tasty for us.

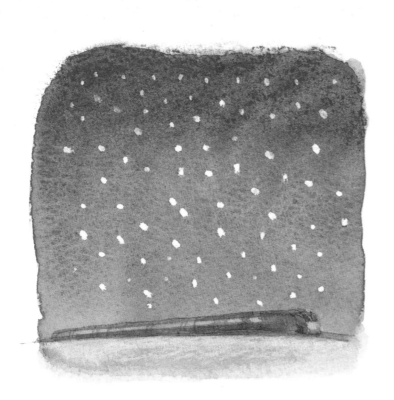

One evening when the man came down from the whirlwind, the world was white. We waited for him as usual but man-cubs began throwing white stuff at us.

The man ran to stop them, but slipped and fell. The man-cubs laughed and crowded around him, snatched his bag and looked inside. Then they threw it on the ground.

Father raced forwards and we followed. I thought Father was going for the food, but he snarled and showed his teeth, so we did the same and chased the man-cubs off into the darkness.

The man was still lying on the icy ground and I licked his hand. Father licked his face.

Then, another whirlwind arrived and people came. From the dark we watched as the man was carried away to a bright flashing light.

We waited for the man the next evening. He didn't come, but I saw one of the man-cubs standing in the shadows. There was no sign of the man on the following evening, but the man-cub came out from the shadows towards us.

We showed him our teeth and he stopped. Then he placed a bag on the ground and backed away into the mist. Father darted forwards and brought the bag back to us. It was full of food. After that, the man-cub came each evening and left food for us. We didn't go close to him because we had seen he was wild.

Then, one evening, the
man came back. He waved
and we went out to meet
him. He had brought all
our favourites.

I saw the man-cub in the
shadows and trotted
towards him but he placed
a bag on the ground, then
backed away.

Now I am bigger, I hunt on my own.
The man still meets Father, and I meet
the man-cub. He doesn't hunt with the
wild pack any more. He is my friend.

We eat under the stars
and watch the whirlwinds go by.